Dear Parents and Educators,

Welcome to Penguin Young Readers! As parents and educators, you know that each child develops at his or her own pace—in terms of speech, critical thinking, and, of course, reading. Penguin Young Readers recognizes this fact. As a result, each Penguin Young Readers book is assigned a traditional easy-to-read level (1–4) as well as a Guided Reading Level (A–P). Both of these systems will help you choose the right book for your child. Please refer to the back of each book for specific leveling information. Penguin Young Readers features esteemed authors and illustrators, stories about favorite characters, fascinating nonfiction, and more!

The Giant Jelly Bean Jar

LEVEL 3

GUIDED READING LEVEL **J**

This book is perfect for a **Transitional Reader** who:
- can read multisyllable and compound words;
- can read words with prefixes and suffixes;
- is able to identify story elements (beginning, middle, end, plot, setting, characters, problem, solution); and
- can understand different points of view.

Here are some **activities** you can do during and after reading this book:
- Character's Feelings: In this story, Ben experiences many feelings, from nervousness to disappointment to excitement. Reread the story and identify the parts where Ben experiences these feelings. Would you feel the same way as Ben? Why or why not?
- Creative Writing: In this story, Jo-Jo gives the kids a weekly jelly bean riddle. Write some of your own riddles. Then try them on your friends.

Remember, sharing the love of reading with a child is the best gift you can give!

—Bonnie Bader, EdM
   Penguin Young Readers program

*Penguin Young Readers are leveled by independent reviewers applying the standards developed by Irene Fountas and Gay Su Pinnell in *Matching Books to Readers: Using Leveled Books in Guided Reading*, Heinemann, 1999.

For my mother, with much love always—MA

For Emily and Bob—PB

Penguin Young Readers
Published by the Penguin Group
Penguin Group (USA) Inc., 375 Hudson Street, New York, New York 10014, USA
Penguin Group (Canada), 90 Eglinton Avenue East, Suite 700, Toronto, Ontario M4P 2Y3, Canada
(a division of Pearson Penguin Canada Inc.)
Penguin Books Ltd, 80 Strand, London WC2R 0RL, England
Penguin Ireland, 25 St Stephen's Green, Dublin 2, Ireland (a division of Penguin Books Ltd)
Penguin Group (Australia), 707 Collins Street, Melbourne, Victoria 3008, Australia
(a division of Pearson Australia Group Pty Ltd)
Penguin Books India Pvt Ltd, 11 Community Centre, Panchsheel Park, New Delhi—110 017, India
Penguin Group (NZ), 67 Apollo Drive, Rosedale, Auckland 0632, New Zealand
(a division of Pearson New Zealand Ltd)
Penguin Books, Rosebank Office Park, 181 Jan Smuts Avenue, Parktown North 2193, South Africa
Penguin China, B7 Jaiming Center, 27 East Third Ring Road North,
Chaoyang District, Beijing 100020, China

Penguin Books Ltd, Registered Offices: 80 Strand, London WC2R 0RL, England

The Library of Congress has cataloged the Dutton edition under the following Control Number:
2004300475
ISBN 978-0-14-240049-4   10 9 8 7 6 5 4 3 2

The Giant Jelly Bean Jar

by Marcie Aboff
pictures by Paige Billin-Frye

Penguin Young Readers
An Imprint of Penguin Group (USA) Inc.

Ben loved jelly beans.

He loved going

to Jo-Jo's Jelly Bean Shop.

Every weekend Jo-Jo had a contest.

Jo-Jo read a riddle and said,

"Guess which jelly bean flavor

is the answer to my riddle."

The person with the right answer

won a jar full of jelly beans.

Every Saturday Ben went

to Jo-Jo's shop with his sister, Jill.

"Yum," Ben said.

"Today I am going to win that jar."

"You say that every week," Jill said.

It was hard to win the prize.

You had to say the answer

in a loud voice.

You had to say it in front of everyone

in the store!

Ben always knew the answer
to Jo-Jo's riddles.
But he never won the jelly beans.

"You are too shy," Jill said every week. She told him to raise his hand high and to speak up.

"Okay," said Ben quietly.

Inside Jo-Jo's shop, Ben and Jill

passed jars and jars

full of jelly beans.

There were apple jelly beans,

bubble gum jelly beans,

and grape jam jelly beans.

There were even popcorn jelly beans!

Jo-Jo stepped out from behind
the counter.

"Hello, my friends!" he called out.

The kids cheered.

"Here is this week's
jelly bean riddle," Jo-Jo said.

"I'm a long yellow fruit
with skin you peel back.
I'm tasty with breakfast,
and I make a great snack!"

Kids waved their hands high in the air.

Ben saw Jill raise her hand.

He raised his hand, too.

But he was very nervous.

He saw bigger kids.

He heard louder kids.

Ben lowered his hand.

Jo-Jo looked at the children.

He pointed to Jill.

"Banana!" Jill cried.

"You are right!" Jo-Jo said.

"We have a jelly bean princess!"

"Oh, nuts!" Ben said to himself.

"I knew the answer, too!"

"Here, Ben," Jill said.

She gave him some jelly beans.

"I'll share my prize with you."

Ben did not say anything.

He wanted to answer

the jelly bean riddle himself.

The next Saturday, Ben and Jill
went back to Jo-Jo's shop.
"Who is ready to be
this week's winner?" Jo-Jo asked.
Everyone cheered.
"Guess this jelly bean flavor," Jo-Jo said.
"I am a big round pie
with cheese and sauce, too.
A slice would be nice—
how many for you?"

Jill whispered, "Go for it, Ben!"

Ben raised his hand.

This time he did not lower it.

But there was another boy
whose hand was higher.

Jo-Jo pointed to that boy instead of Ben.

"Pizza!" the boy shouted.

"Right!" Jo-Jo said.

"Here is a jelly bean jar
for my new jelly bean prince."

"Oh, nuts!" Ben said to himself.

"Not again!"

Ben and Jill walked home together.

"Don't worry, Ben," Jill said.

"Next time you'll win for sure."

The next Saturday, Ben and Jill
went to Jo-Jo's shop again.
But this week was different.
It was special.
Jo-Jo's Jelly Bean Shop had been
open for one year.
Jo-Jo was having a big party.

The store was more crowded than ever.

Jo-Jo stepped out from
behind the counter.
He raised a very, very big jar
of jelly beans over his head.
Everyone cheered.

"Who will be my Grand Prize
winner today?" he asked.
Kids waved their hands high.
"Me, me!" they called out.

Ben just looked at the jelly bean jar.

It was the biggest jar

he had ever seen!

He listened carefully to Jo-Jo's riddle.

"I'm yummy with jelly
and can be spooned from a jar.
Between slices of bread
I'm a true sandwich star!"

Ben knew the answer right away.

This time he lifted his hand high.

Then he looked at the jar again.

He raised his hand a little higher.

Then he raised it as high as he could.

He even stood on his tippy-toes!

Jo-Jo looked out at the big crowd.

He pointed to Ben.

Ben was so surprised,

he forgot the answer

to the riddle!

Everyone waited for Ben to speak.

But he didn't say anything.

Some people started to wave

their hands again.

"Me, me!" they shouted.

Ben still did not say anything.

Jill looked at the crowd.

Then she looked at Ben.

She lifted up her foot.

She stepped right on Ben's toes.

"OH, NUTS!" Ben cried out.

Nuts, Ben thought.

"Peanuts," he whispered.

Then Ben remembered

the answer to the riddle.

In a big voice, he yelled,

"Yes!" Jill shouted.

"Yes!" Jo-Jo cried.

Jo-Jo placed a sparkling crown
on Ben's head.

He handed Ben the great
big jelly bean prize jar.

"How does it feel to be
the Grand Prize Jelly Bean King?"
Jill asked Ben.
"Great!" Ben said, loud and clear.
He did not feel one bit nervous.

On the way home,

Jill patted Ben on the back.

"You did it!" she said.

Ben grinned.

"Thank you for stepping

on my toes!" he said.

Jill grinned back.

"That's what sisters are for!"